There's a Troll at the Bottom of Our Street!

Ann Jungman

Illustrated by Doffy Weir

HAPPY CAT BOOKS

To Natasha with love

Published by
Happy Cat Books
An imprint of Catnip Publishing Ltd
Islington Business Centre
3-5 Islington High Street
London N1 9LQ

This edition first published 2006
1 3 5 7 9 10 8 6 4 2

Text copyright © Ann Jungman, 1996
Illustrations copyright © Doffy Weir, 1996
The moral rights of the author and illustrator have been asserted

ISBN 10: 1 905117 15 9
ISBN 13: 978-1-905117-15-4

There's a Troll at the Bottom of Our Street!

Contents

The Adventure

The children of Sebastopol
Avenue were bored. They
were very, very bored.

"I wish the summer holiday
didn't go on for so long,"
moaned Patrick.

"Me, too," agreed Darren.

"I wish the troll would play with us more often," sniffed Selima. "Like he used to in the old days."

"Let's see if he's awake,"
suggested Darren.

So the three children went to
the troll's shed at the bottom
of the garden. They were just

about to knock when they saw
the big notice on the door.

10

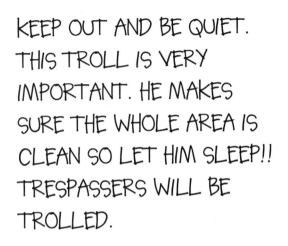

KEEP OUT AND BE QUIET.
THIS TROLL IS VERY
IMPORTANT. HE MAKES
SURE THE WHOLE AREA IS
CLEAN SO LET HIM SLEEP!!
TRESPASSERS WILL BE
TROLLED.

"Oh dear," said Selima.
"We'd better leave our troll alone."

"What's that about me?" came a sleepy voice and the troll opened the door, yawning and rubbing his eyes.

"We're bored," the children told him.

"You're always bored,"

grumbled the troll. "Well, you can come and help me sort out the rubbish that's piling up again."

"Oh no," complained the children. "We want to do something different."

"All right," said the troll,

"I'll take you all out. We'll
go exploring and have a very
special adventure."

"We haven't got any
money," groaned the children.

"You don't need any money
to have an adventure," said
the troll disapprovingly.

"Come on and I'll show you
the very special troll way not
to be bored."

The three children and the
troll walked to the end of the
street and looked over the
bridge into the canal below.

"Hmm," said the troll. "I've never been down by the canal. How do we get in?"

"We're not supposed to go in," Selima told him. "It's all locked up."

"We must be able to get in

somehow," insisted the troll, "Let's go and look. It's all right, you're with me. Now come on."

So they wandered past some old warehouses and eventually the troll found a gap in the fence through which he could climb on to the tow-path by the canal.

"Come on in," he called over the fence to the children. "I'll hold the gap open."

So one by one the children crawled through the hole.

On both sides of the canal grass and weeds had grown so high they almost covered the

path and the canal was brown
and grim, covered with green
sludge, and there was a rusted
old pram and lots of rubbish
sticking out above the water.

"It's not very nice here,"
commented Selima.

"You don't know," argued

the troll. "Let's just walk along for a bit. Who knows what we may find?"

The children walked behind the troll trying to ignore the smell coming from the canal.

"I think we should be getting back," commented

Darren. "It looks as though it's going to rain."

"Yes," agreed Patrick quickly. "The sky is getting very dark."

"Nonsense!" replied the troll. "I promised you an adventure and an adventure is what you are going to have."

They rounded a bend and saw a small metal bridge that crossed the canal from one

side to the other. The troll
looked at it and a tear ran
down his face.

"What's up?" asked Selima.

"It reminds me of my
rickedy, rackedy bridge,"

howled the troll and he got out
his hanky and blew his nose
hard.

The children crowded round
him and patted him on the
back and wondered what to

do. Suddenly Darren smiled
broadly. "I've got a brilliant
idea," he informed the others.

"All right, genius, what is
it?" demanded Selima.

"The troll can go and sit

under the bridge and we can all pretend to be the Three Billy Goats Gruff," explained Darren.

The troll grinned and dried his tears and ran over the bridge and disappeared under

it. Then the children heard
him say: "Who's that going
trippidy, trap across my
rickedy rackedy bridge?"

"It is I, little Billy Goat
Gruff," squeaked Selima,
"Can I come across, please?"

"No!"
"I'm a troll, fol-de-rol,
I'm a troll, fol-de-rol,
I'm a troll, fol-de-rol,
   And I'll eat you for my
supper."

The children and the troll
all shrieked with laughter.
And then a wild scream rang
out from somewhere near the
bridge. They all froze with
horror.

The Rickedy, Rackedy Bridge

The troll and the three
children stared at each other.
Then the troll began to shake
and cry.

"It's the Three Billy Goats
Gruff," he wept. "They have
come to haunt me. Help, help!
I've got to get away," and the
troll, his eyes wild with fear,
began to climb up the slope
next to the canal. The troll was

almost on the path when he slipped and fell into the canal, s-p-l-a-s-h!

"Help," shrieked the troll, "I can't swim."

Darren ran over the bridge and grabbed the troll and pulled him out of the water.

"Quick," said Patrick, "let's get out of here," as another of the strange screams rang out.

The three children dragged the troll over the bridge and towards the hole they had used to get in. A few minutes later they stood on the street. Darren and the troll were dripping wet. Fortunately, the

milkman was driving past in his milk cart.

"What happened to you lot, then?" he asked.

"The troll fell into the canal and Darren rescued him," Selima told him.

"Huh," commented

the milkman. "You smell disgusting, you two, but you'll catch your death of cold standing there. Come on, get into the cart and I'll drive you home."

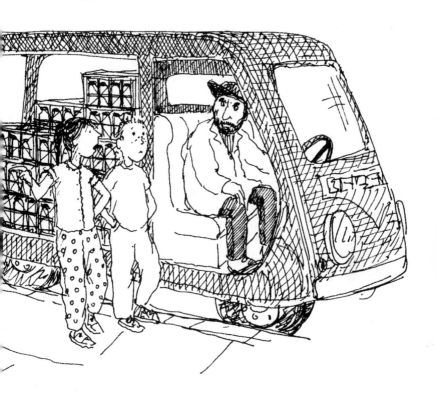

So Darren and the troll sat on the back of the cart among the crates and the milk bottles. The troll stared straight ahead muttering: "They've come to haunt me, my life will never be the same again," and he buried his face in his hands.

When the milk cart dropped them off, Darren's mother came running out. "Look at you two, soaking wet. What have you been doing? Come in the back way and take off those wet clothes in the kitchen, and straight into the bath."

Half an hour later Darren and the troll came downstairs. Darren tucked into the food that Mrs Brook put in front of him but the troll refused everything, even chocolate

chip ice-cream. He sat huddled in a blanket shaking.

"I'm going to call an ambulance," said Mrs Brook. "I think he's got a fever and should be in hospital." So the

troll was taken to hospital and
the residents of Sebastopol
Avenue took it in turns to
sit by his bed all day and all
night. The troll just lay there,
and shook and mumbled to
himself.

"He's got a very high

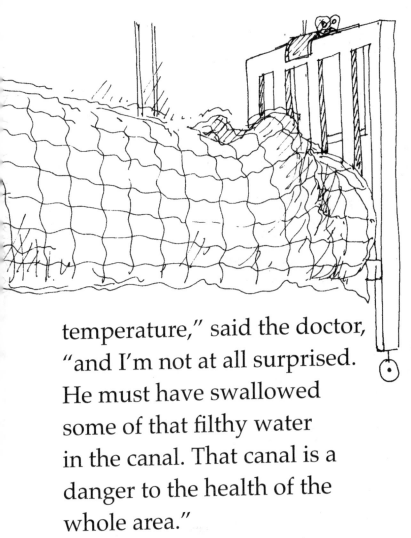

temperature," said the doctor,
"and I'm not at all surprised.
He must have swallowed
some of that filthy water
in the canal. That canal is a
danger to the health of the
whole area."

That evening, while the

children sat with the troll,
their parents all got together.

"That canal is a disgrace,"
said Darren's dad. "We've got
to get it cleaned up."

"I agree," said Mrs Singh.
"The fences are not enough

to keep the children out. It's
a danger to all the children in
the area."

"And it attracts flies in the
summer," chipped in Mr
Gorman. "We've got to get the
council to clean it up."

"We'll start a campaign,"
said Mr Singh. "And when
the troll is better he can give
interviews to the local paper."

"Yes!" said Mrs Brook.
"Everyone likes to read

about trolls, we'll get lots of publicity."

"He might even get on TV," cried Mrs Gorman. "I'm going to enjoy this campaign, I know I am."

The Ghosts

A week went by but the troll did not get any better.

"I can't understand it," the doctor told the children. "His temperature has gone down, but he just lies there and looks at the ceiling."

The children stood round the troll's bed and looked miserable. Patrick had brought a brand new kind of ice-cream: coconut and praline with chocolate. Each of the children took a spoonful and agreed it was the best ice-cream ever.

"Why don't you try a spoonful?" Patrick asked the troll desperately. "You'd love it."

But the troll just went on staring miserably at the ceiling.

After a few days he was moved into a room on his

own because he was having
nightmares and shouting in
his sleep.

"Something about his
having been very bad and

46

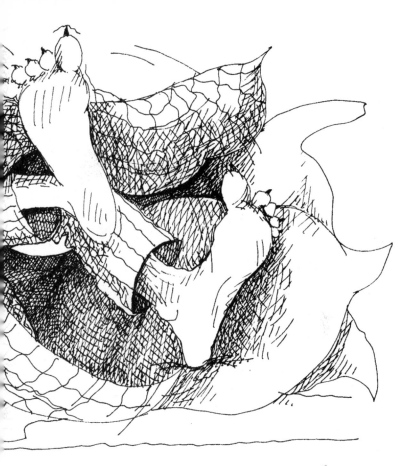

Three Billy Goats Gruff," the
doctor told the children.

Patrick and Selima and
Darren suddenly realized
what the problem was.

"It was the shriek under the bridge, he really believes that it was the ghosts of the Billy Goats Gruff," cried Darren.

"I see," said the doctor. "So that poor old troll thinks that ghosts from his past have come back to haunt him."

"Right," agreed Darren.
"Make the sound you heard
under the bridge," demanded
the doctor.

"It was really horrible," cried Patrick.

"Really scary," agreed Selima. "Like a mad thing from another world."

And the children took it in turns to imitate the ghostly noise. The troll put his head under the sheet and began to cry.

"It was only us," cried the children. "Oh, poor troll, please don't be upset."

"Come on," said the doctor. "Take me to that rickedy, rackedy bridge. We're going to get to the bottom of this."

So the doctor and the

51

children made their way to the
canal and found the hole in
the fence.

"We promised we wouldn't
ever go there again," said
Selima.

"And we're scared," added
Patrick.

"I'm surprised at you," said
the doctor. "I thought the troll
was your friend."

"That's true," nodded
Darren. "We've got to go back
there and find out what is
really going on and help our
troll get better."

"Yes, and I'm sure your parents would make an exception just this once. After all, this time you're with a responsible adult."

The four of them found the bridge and walked across, and the same creepy sound rang out. The children went white and got ready to run.

"I think I've found the cause of all the problems," said the doctor and he pointed under the bridge. The three children peered nervously into the darkness. Eight green eyes stared back at them.

"It's an eight-eyed monster," shrieked Patrick. "Let's get out of here!"

The Canal

"Look again," said the doctor.
As their eyes got used to the
dark they saw a cat with three
kittens.

"She's a wild cat," the
doctor told them. "When she
heard you messing around
she was frightened for her
kittens."

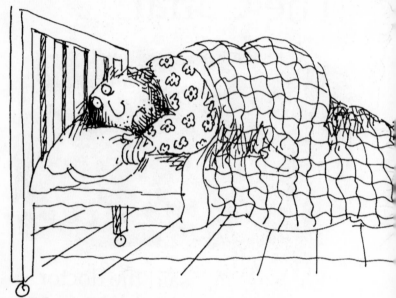

The children laughed and
went to stroke the cat.

"No, don't," said the doctor.
"She's wild and isn't used to
people, she'll scratch. We'll
have to get to know her
slowly, build up her trust."

So twice a day the children

fed the cat and gradually she
let them stroke her.

One day they took the cat
and her kittens in a big
basket to the hospital. The
troll was still lying silently in
his bed.

"Well, troll," the doctor told

him. "We have brought your ghosts to see you!"

"No!" shrieked the troll, burying himself under the sheets again, his teeth chattering. The doctor put the

cats on the bed. The kittens
began to walk all over the
troll, miaowing loudly.

The doctor and the children
watched the troll anxiously.
First his teeth stopped

chattering, then the shaking stopped, and suddenly his head popped out from under his sheets.

"Your ghosts," said the doctor smiling.

"They're lovely," said the troll, stroking the black-and-white kittens. 'Were they under the rickedy, rackedy bridge?"

"They certainly were."

"You're not just saying that?"

"No!" cried the children, "We found them there. The mother cat was wild but she got used to us."

"Well," said the troll, sitting up. "Where's my ice-cream? I'm starving, absolutely starving."

Once the press heard the troll was better they wanted to interview him.

"No one is to say anything
about me being scared of
ghosts," said the troll. "I want
you all to promise never to
say anything to anyone about
it. My troll image would
suffer a lot if people knew that

I had been scared by a cat and some kittens."

So smiling to themselves, they all promised the troll.

"That canal made me very ill," he informed the reporters, "very ill indeed and I think something should be done about it."

That week the local papers carried headlines like "CLEAN UP CANAL SAYS TROLL" and "TROLL SAYS CANAL A DANGER TO THE COMMUNITY".

As soon as the troll was back at work he started a campaign to clean up the canal.

"There's a march tonight!" he would tell people as he organised the rubbish. "Don't forget to come."

Everyone did come and the biggest crowd anyone could remember stood outside the town hall demanding something be done about the canal.

"We'd like to clean up the canal, really we would," the Mayor told the troll. "But we just don't have enough

money. We're as worried as you are about the health problems the canal poses, but we just can't undertake such a big task."

So the march broke up and everyone went home feeling rather miserable.

Troll's Lock

That evening the Brooks
and the Gormans and the
Singhs had dinner together to
welcome the troll back. When
the meal was over they drank
a toast to the troll.

"Welcome back to Sebastopol Avenue – we all missed you."

The troll stood, wiped the ice-cream from his face and began to make a speech: "Unaccustomed as I am to public speaking, I would just

like to thank you for this
splendid dinner and your
wonderful support while I
was ill in the hospital, and –"

At that moment the phone
rang.

"It's for the troll," said Mrs
Brook. "It's a TV
company.

They want to interview you
on television about the canal."
"Television," cried the
troll, his eyes growing big

with amazement. "Me, on television. Oh no, I couldn't, I'd be too scared."

"But what about the dangers of the canal?" insisted Selima. "You've got to go, you could make all the difference."

The troll shook his head. "Can't," he whispered. "Too scared."

"We'll go with you," offered the children. "Would that help?"

The troll nodded and took the phone from Mrs Brook.

"Hello, Mr Television," he said nervously. "Mr Troll speaking. I am willing to be on your show, but only if my friends can come too."

So the next day the troll and the three children sat in a TV studio.

The troll began to shake and Selima held his hand.

"Now, Mr Troll, would you like to tell the viewers about your terrible experience after

falling into the canal?" asked
the interviewer.

"I was ill," mumbled the
troll. "Very, very ill."

"Yes, he was," agreed

78

Selima. "He had a very high temperature."

"And a terrible fever," added Patrick.

"He was in hospital for weeks," volunteered Darren.

"So you all think the canal

is a great danger to public health?"

"Definitely," they all cried.

Soon after that the Mayor came to visit the troll at the rubbish-sorting plant.

"Great news, troll," he called up to the troll. "A big group of people want to clean up our canal and then turn it into a leisure space."

"A what?" asked the troll,
climbing down.

"A leisure space. You know, for boating and canoeing, walking and cycling, and a market, and trips up and down the canal telling people about its history."

"Would that be good?" asked the troll.

"Good? It would be wonderful. Lots of jobs while the canal is being developed and then people coming into the area to enjoy the canal and spend money and something for us to enjoy too. Oh, I'm so excited and none of it would have happened without you!" And the Mayor

kissed the troll on both
cheeks.

When all the work was
finished the canal was opened.
A huge crowd turned up for

the Gala opening. The troll
and the children sat on the
platform with the Mayor and
the actress who was opening
the new lock. There was
a big band and streamers
everywhere. The canal was
full of boats of every kind, all
decorated and full of people.

"It is with great pleasure
that I declare this wonderful
new public space open,"

declared the actress. "The local people have decided to call it 'Troll's Lock' and I for one am looking forward to spending a lot of time here," and she cut the ribbon and opened the lock.

All day and evening people

sailed up and down, bought
things in the market, ate and
drank, and danced to the
band.

The children were very
good and quiet; no one could
understand where they were.
Then there was a break in the

music and everyone could hear floating through the summer night, "Who's that going trippedy, trap over my rickedy, rackedy bridge?"

"Oh, that's all right," said the parents. "The children are all playing with the troll. And that is exactly as it should be at 'Troll's Lock'."

Beware of the Troll!
Actually, you're quite safe because this troll doesn't eat goats or
people. He prefers ice-cream. When Selima, Darren and Patrick
find a troll crying in the garden shed, they don't know what to
do or what to tell their parents. It looks as if life will never be the
same again for the residents of Sebastopol Avenue!

Ann Jungman

There's a Troll at the Top of Our Tip!

Beware, unemployed Troll!
Troll loves his job at the tip and is devastated to discover he is
no longer required. But he is a popular troll and the children of
Sebastopol Avenue work tirelessly to get him his job back. That's
what friends are for!

Ann Jungman
Broomstick Services

When Mabel and her sister Ethel decide they've had enough of being witches, they plan to set up a new business. Broomstick Services will make deliveries to everyone on the estate and children Jackie, Lucy and Joe will help them do it. The only problem is the other sister, Maud. She's a very bad witch with no plans to retire and she could ruin everything.

Ann Jungman

Broomstick Removals

Mabel and Ethel have no hope of running Broomstick Services if they can't find their broomsticks. Something must be done and fast, but what? Sister Maud used to be a bad witch, until she settled down and got married. Can they persuade her to jump on her broomstick one more time?

Ann Jungman

Broomstick Rescues

Mabel and Ethel can't wait to go on holiday and forget about work for a while. But even at the seaside, they can't put their feet up. There are holidaymakers in trouble and our warm-hearted witches must hurry to rescue them!

Mabel and Ethel's sister, Maud, has had a baby girl and she's
determined that little Tracey Sharon will not become a witch.
However, magic is in the baby's blood and it's not long before
things start to happen...